Text copyright © Anthony Masters 2000
Illustrations copyright © Alan Marks 2000

First published in Great Britain in 2000
by Wayland, an imprint of
Hachette Children's Book

Reprinted in 2006 and 2007 Wayland
is an imprint of Hachette Children's Books, an
Hachette Livre UK Company.

The right of Anthony Masters to be identified as
the authorand Alan Marks the illustrator of this
Work has been asserted by them in accordance
with the Copyright, Designs and Patents Act 1988

Printed in China

British Library Cataloguing in Publication Data
available

ISBN-13: 978 0 7502 5031 3

Wayland
338 Euston Road, London NW1 3BH

ANTHONY MASTERS

BEWARE THE WICKED WEB

Illustrated by Alan Marks

WAYLAND

Chapter One

The rustling was much louder as Rob and Sam climbed the stairs to the attic, but when they arrived at the top, all they could see was darkness. Sam swept the attic with her torch beam. The space was completely empty but they could still hear the silky rustling that had kept them awake all night.

Rob shivered. "What is it?" he asked
once again.

"How would I know?" snapped Sam.

She shone her torch around the dusty
walls of the attic until the heavy oak door
was caught in the beam. "I think it's coming
from behind that door."

"There must be another room in there,"
whispered Rob.

"Let's go in," said Sam.

"Wait a minute." Rob hesitated.

Sam had always been the adventurous one. Although he was a year older, her brother, Rob, was more cautious. Now, with his mass of dark hair and pale face, he looked downright terrified.

Sam wasn't feeling so good herself. But she was the one who always wanted to make decisions. It didn't matter whether they were right or wrong.

"There's no *point* in waiting," she said briskly.

"But that rustling sound... Suppose it's dangerous?" asked Rob, nervously.

"Well, there's only one way to find out..." Sam gave the door a push and it opened without a sound.

"Shine the torch then," hissed Rob.

The beam swept the inside of the room. Rob gasped and Sam screamed.

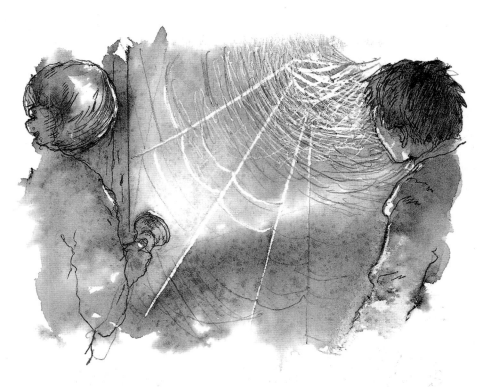

Right in front of them were the dusty, rustling folds of the most enormous cobweb they had ever seen.

Where was the spider? wondered Rob, cold shock waves spreading inside him.

"I'm not going in there," said Sam.

Rob was taken by surprise. Sam went everywhere. She never chickened out. Now it looked as if he was going to have to take charge and go in first.

But what urged Rob on was the small black book propped up against a cushion on the web-shrouded table.

He had the oddest feeling that it had been put there for a reason.

"The book—" Rob began.

"What?"

"On the table. It looks... important."

"Does it?" Sam swept the beam around the room again and suddenly realized she was peering into the dusty remains of a child's bedroom. There was a small bed against the wall, a table and an oil lamp. On the cobweb-matted walls were pictures of animals and on the floor was a half-open box of old-fashioned-looking toys, a teddy bear and a wooden train.

Although there was no sign of an open
window, the web was rustling as if in a light
breeze.

"It's throbbing," murmured Sam, as she
watched the folds move in a kind of rhythm.
She shuddered and tried to step back, but
Rob was blocking the doorway.

"Can you see the egg?" Rob asked quietly, his voice trembling.

"What egg?" whispered Sam.

"Up there. Above the bed. Between the wall and the ceiling."

The egg was as big as a football, wrapped tightly in a fluffy cocoon.

"Whatever laid that?" she asked, hardly able to get out the words. Sam was trembling all over and when she glanced at Rob she could see he was shaking too.

"A spider?"

"That size?"

"Maybe it's a *big* spider," Rob replied, panic sweeping through him.

Chapter Two

Thankfully, there was no sign of any spider as Sam's beam swept the room again and again.

Rob wheeled round. "Look at that lot."

Part of the web near the egg was covered in the black bodies of dead flies.

"How did they get in?" Sam demanded.

"Check out the ceiling again," said Rob.

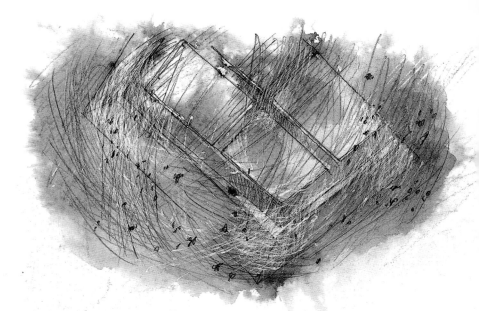

Eventually Sam's torch lit a skylight window, covered in web but open a fraction.

"That must be where the breeze is coming from," she said, sounding relieved.

"And the flies," added Rob. Then he shook himself and stared towards the table.

"I want that book," he said with surprising determination.

"Why?"

"It might tell us something. I've got this hunch."

Sam groaned. Rob often had hunches.

"Let's get a broom and push the web out of the way," she suggested. "Then you can grab your precious book."

Hurrying downstairs and just managing to avoid their mother, Sam and Rob grabbed two brooms from the kitchen cupboard and hurried back to the attic.

"Something's changed," whispered Rob.

To their amazement they saw that strands of the web were rustling around the heavy oak door.

"It couldn't be growing, could it?"

"No chance," snapped Sam. "We must have pulled out those strands when we closed the door. Didn't we?" she added, doubtfully.

Chapter Three

Slowly, Rob went into the attic bedroom.

Sam followed. She was surprised. Rob only ever took the lead if he wanted something badly. Why should he so desperately want that mouldy old book?

She shuddered as she touched the soft grey folds of rustling web. Sam hadn't realized they would be so sticky – or so clinging.

"Use your broom," hissed Rob. "Push the thing aside."

It was like sweeping away a living creature, for as soon as they brushed them aside the folds flopped back, sticky and suffocating. Rob leant over, wrenching the little black book from a fold of the web, which made a slurping, sucking sound.

"Got it!"

"Let's get out of here." Sam shuddered again as the strands of web caught at her in a strong and sticky grip. Pulling away hard, she ran for the door, with Rob close behind, clutching the book.

Once in his own bedroom, Rob pulled an old football shirt out of a drawer and rubbed away at the mouldy book, making flakes of the leather cover fly in the air.

As he worked, Sam thought back to last week when they had only just moved into number 14, one of a row of four-storey houses along the river where the wharves had once been. Next door was an old fruit warehouse that their parents had bought and planned to turn into flats.

"I'm going to make the attic into a big games room for both of you," Dad had promised. "But don't go up there yet. No one's used it for years and it could be dangerous."

He can say that again, thought Sam. Should they tell him? Then she remembered how much trouble they'd be in for being in the attic in the first place.

Sam wished they had never gone up there at all. She remembered the toys and wondered why a child had been sleeping in that tiny attic space. There were plenty of other rooms in the house.

"It's a diary," said Rob, finally able to prise open the cover. He paused. "But there's only one entry." He began to read aloud:

"July 4th. My name is Abby Hall. Since my parents died, Aunt Grace has been horrible to me. Sometimes I think she wants me to die up here. If I did die, Aunt Grace would inherit my fortune. She told me I've got to stay in this attic until I've learnt to be a good girl. She says the web is only in my imagination. But I can see the web growing every day and it's not just the web that's growing. The spider is, too."

Underneath, Abby had drawn a picture of an enormous spider.

His heart pounding, Rob showed the drawing to Sam. "That's no ordinary spider," he said. "It's tropical."

"Oh, really?" scoffed Sam. "And how do you think a tropical spider could have got up here?"

Chapter Four

That afternoon, Rob and Sam went to the
library to look at some books on insects.
After a long search they found a picture
of Abby's spider, with a chilling description.

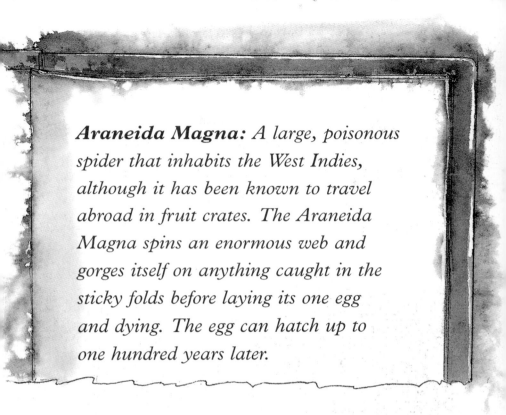

Araneida Magna: *A large, poisonous spider that inhabits the West Indies, although it has been known to travel abroad in fruit crates. The Araneida Magna spins an enormous web and gorges itself on anything caught in the sticky folds before laying its one egg and dying. The egg can hatch up to one hundred years later.*

"But I don't understand. How could a giant poisonous spider from the West Indies get into that attic?" asked Sam uneasily.

"What about the warehouse next door?" asked Rob. "Wasn't it used to store bananas, a long time ago? Maybe Aunt Grace got to hear about an *Araneida Magna* turning up at the warehouse and bribed someone to smuggle the spider into the attic."

"Is *that* why Abby wrote up her diary, as a warning?" Sam and Rob looked at each other in mounting horror.

Then Rob said, "We've got to destroy that egg right away. It could hatch any minute."

They were shivering with fear and anxiety as they once again climbed the attic stairs.

At the top, Sam switched on the torch.

"The web's grown again," she gasped.

This time, even more strands were wrapped tightly around the door to the bedroom, quivering and rustling much more strongly than before. Sam picked up one of the brooms and began to sweep at the silky folds. But this time they didn't come away so easily and she found the broom was getting furred up, its bristles sticking to the strands of the web.

Rob picked up the other broom and began to help, but they made slow progress.

"It's like trying to brush away treacle," he said breathlessly.

"The strands are thicker and stickier," Sam said in horror. "It's as if they're trying to trap us."

Chapter Five

Sam and Rob finally managed to part the web and push open the door.

Inside the attic room, the silky strands had grown so thickly that the beam of Sam's torch could hardly penetrate the sticky tangle and they could only just make out the egg above Abby's bed.

"If that thing hatches, we could be the next victims," whispered Sam bleakly.

They began to hack away at the folds of the web, but the silky stickiness only wrapped itself around the brooms again, rather like grey candyfloss. Sam and Rob gave out cries of disgust.

Worse still, the throbbing was much stronger, much more like a heartbeat, thought Sam.

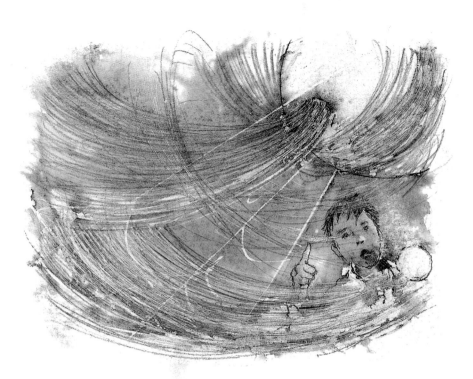

Then she saw that Rob had grabbed the torch and was pointing up at the egg with a shaking finger.

Now they had hacked away so much they could see that one strand of the web had plugged into the fluffy cocoon.

"The web's *feeding* the egg," hissed Rob. "We've got to destroy it – fast. Can't you see? It's not just the web that's pulsating, it's the egg, too."

With renewed determination, Rob and
Sam attacked the sticky folds, pushing the
web away until a tunnel was formed – a
tunnel that led to Abby's bed, just below
the pulsating, vibrating egg.

"Who's going through?" asked Rob.
"There isn't room for us both or we'll get
caught in the sticky stuff."

Sam hesitated.

"Come on!" said Rob. "We haven't got
time to hang around."

"OK," she replied reluctantly. "Let's toss for it." Sam dragged a coin out of her jeans and spun it awkwardly in the enclosed space, which seemed to be getting smaller all the time as the web spun itself back together again. "Heads or tails?" she asked.

"Heads!"

The coin spun. The web spun. The coin turned up tails.

"Wish me luck," said Rob miserably.

Chapter Six

Ducking down, Rob began to edge his way along the tunnel which was closing in on them all the time, clutching the broom in both hands.

Terrified, Sam watched him, her torch beam picking out the hundreds of dead flies caught in the web.

"Look out!" she yelled as some strands seemed to reach out towards Rob. Then suddenly the folds of the web began to wrap themselves around him, strand after strand, coil after coil of sticky grey silk.

"Help!" Rob's voice sounded smothered already as the coils tightened. "It's squeezing me!"

"I'm coming!" Sam began to hit out at the strands with her broom, working faster and more furiously than she had ever done before, pushing back the folds until she reached her brother.

As Sam tore with her bare hands at the web that was squeezing Rob, the strands tried to wrap themselves around her as well.

"Leave me!" gasped Rob. "Go for the egg."

"No way."

"You've got to. Look at it. I'm sure it's beginning to hatch!" He yelled out in pain as the coils tightened yet again.

Sam glanced up at the egg. It was pulsating hard now and there were splits in its fluffy grey surface.

She leapt forward, her broom wrestling
with the web, raising it above her head, the
coils clutching.

Sam tore the broom away and jumped up on Abby's bed. The rusty springs screamed but the egg was just within reach.

Looking round her, Sam saw the web was growing back faster than ever, the deadly strands reaching out to her.

"Go for it!" gasped Rob, his voice faint. "You've got to destroy the egg."

Without hesitation, Sam brushed a path across the ceiling with the broom to reach the egg. Tightening her grip, she rammed the head of the broom as hard as she could into the egg. Something dropped on to her head and she let out a shrill scream.

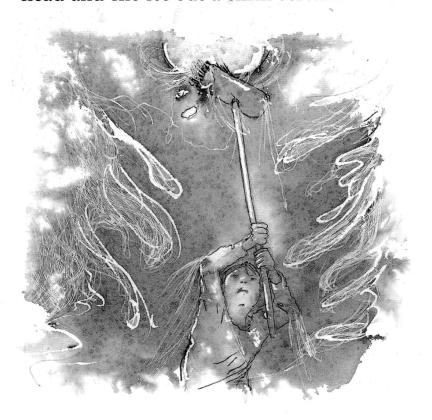

But instead of a writhing, leggy spider, a torrent of black dust had covered Sam from top to toe. The egg had vanished.

She glanced frantically at Rob. To her relief, the folds of the web were slowly releasing him. As he dragged himself away they let out a sighing, sucking sound.

Rob gazed at the strands that still hung around the walls of Abby's bedroom. They were changing, losing their stickiness, no longer rustling. Instead they were becoming dry and dusty.

"The web's dead," yelled Rob.

Sam was close to tears.

More dust fell, showering them, until Rob was black with the stuff, too.

"There'll be nothing left of the web soon," he whispered.

Rob and Sam turned to the door to see their mother standing there, looking absolutely furious.

"Just *what* do you two think you're doing covered in that filthy black dust? And aren't those my brooms? You were told not to play up here!" She glared at them angrily.

"Sorry," they both mumbled.

Rob had Abby's diary tucked safely in his pocket.

Had it not been for Abby's warning, there was no telling what might have happened.

"I don't know how you can bear to come up here," continued their mother. "This attic could be *swarming* with spiders."

Just one in an egg, thought Sam. But she knew the *Araneida Magna* would have made up for all the rest. There was no point in trying to explain what had happened. Mum would never believe them.

Then something small, dark and furry scurried across the floor towards them and their mother screamed and screamed again. "There you are! Can't you see what I mean?"

"It's only a small one," said Rob.

"Are you expecting anything larger?" demanded Mum sarcastically.

"Not now," he said quietly, winking at Sam.

If you have enjoyed this book, why not try these other creepy titles:

The Claygate Hound by Jan Dean
It's the school trip to Claygate, and Zeb and Ryan are ready to explore, until they hear stories about the ghost in the woods. It all sounds like a stupid story. But then the boys start to see shadows moving in the trees and eyes glistening in the darkness. Could the Claygate Hound really exist?

The Ghosts of Golfhawk School by Tessa Potter
Martin and Dan like to scare others with stories about the ghosts at Golfhawk School. But when Kirsty arrives and strange things start to happen it no longer seems a joke. Can she really see ghostly figures in the playground? And why have students and teachers started to get sick?

Danny and the Sea of Darkness by David Clayton
When does a dream become reality? Danny wakes one night to find himself out at sea during a terrible storm. As he falls overboard into the icy water Danny wonders if he will ever return from the Sea of Darkness.

Time Flies by Mary Hooper
The large oak box looked like the perfect place to hide, but Lucy could never have imagined what powers lay inside. Lucy steps back in time to a strange and scary world. Can she find her way home again before it's too late?

Ghost on the Landing by Eleanor Allen
Jack wakes in the night screaming in fear. His sister's ghost stories about Aunt Stella's spooky old house must have been giving him nightmares. But was it just a bad dream or does the ghost on the landing really exist?